THE MACHINE STOPS

Robinia Classics

Printed or published to the highest ethical standard.

THE MACHINE STOPS

By
E. M. FORSTER

Robinia Classics

UNITED KINGDOM
1909

CONTENTS

THE AIR SHIP

IMAGINE, if you can, a small room, hexagonal in shape, like the cell of a bee. It is lighted neither by window nor by lamp, yet it is filled with a soft radiance. There are no apertures for ventilation, yet the air is fresh. There are no musical instruments, and yet, at the moment that my meditation opens, this room is throbbing with melodious sounds. An armchair is in the centre, by its side a reading-desk – that is all the furniture. And in the armchair there sits a swaddled lump of flesh – a woman, about five feet high, with a face as white as a fungus. It is to her that the little room belongs.

An electric bell rang.

The woman touched a switch and the music was silent.

'I suppose I must see who it is', she thought, and set her chair in motion. The chair, like the music, was worked by machinery and it rolled her to the other side of the room where the bell still rang importunately.

'Who is it?' she called. Her voice was irritable, for she had been interrupted often since the music began. She knew several thousand people, in certain directions human intercourse had advanced enormously.

But when she listened into the receiver, her white face wrinkled into smiles, and she said: 'Very well. Let us talk, I will isolate myself. I do not expect anything important will happen for the next five minutes – for I can give you fully five minutes, Kuno. Then I must deliver my lecture on "Music during the Australian Period".'

She touched the isolation knob, so that no one else could speak to her. Then she touched the lighting apparatus, and the little room was plunged into darkness. 'Be quick!' she called, her irritation returning. 'Be quick, Kuno; here I am in the dark wasting my time.'

But it was fully fifteen seconds before the round plate that she held in her hands began to glow. A faint blue light shot across it, darkening to purple, and presently she could see the image of her son, who lived on the other side of the earth, and he could see her. 'Kuno, how slow you are.'

He smiled gravely.

'I really believe you enjoy dawdling.'

'I have called you before, mother, but you were always busy or isolated. I have something particular to say.'

'What is it, dearest boy? Be quick. Why could you not send it by pneumatic post?'

'Because I prefer saying such a thing. I want----'

'Well?'

'I want you to come and see me.'

Vashti watched his face in the blue plate.

'But I can see you!' she exclaimed. 'What more do you want?'

'I want to see you not through the Machine,' said Kuno. 'I want to speak to you not through the wearisome Machine.'

'Oh, hush!' said his mother, vaguely shocked. 'You mustn't say anything against the Machine.'

'Why not?'

'One mustn't.'

'You talk as if a god had made the Machine,' cried the other.

'I believe that you pray to it when you are unhappy. Men made it, do not forget that. Great men, but men. The Machine is much, but it is not everything. I see something like you in this plate, but I do not see you. I hear something like you through this telephone, but I do not hear you. That is why I want you to come. Pay me a visit, so that we can meet face to face, and talk about the hopes that are in my mind.'

She replied that she could scarcely spare the time for a visit.

'The air-ship barely takes two days to fly between me and you.'

'I dislike air-ships.'

'Why?'

'I dislike seeing the horrible brown earth, and the sea, and the stars when it is dark. I get no ideas in an air-ship.'

'I do not get them anywhere else.'

'What kind of ideas can the air give you?' He paused for an instant.

'Do you not know four big stars that form an oblong, and three stars close together in the middle of the oblong, and hanging from these stars, three other stars?'

'No, I do not. I dislike the stars. But did they give you an idea? How interesting; tell me.'

'I had an idea that they were like a man.'

'I do not understand.'

'The four big stars are the man's shoulders and his knees.

The three stars in the middle are like the belts that men wore once, and the three stars hanging are like a sword.'

'A sword?'

'Men carried swords about with them, to kill animals and other men.'

'It does not strike me as a very good idea, but it is certainly original. When did it come to you first?'

'In the air-ship-----' He broke off, and she fancied that he looked sad. She could not be sure, for the Machine did not transmit nuances of expression. It only gave a general idea of people – an idea that was good enough for all practical purposes, Vashti thought. The imponderable bloom, declared by a discredited philosophy to be the actual essence of intercourse, was rightly ignored by the Machine, just as the imponderable bloom of the grape was ignored by the manufacturers of artificial fruit. Something 'good enough' had long since been accepted by our race.

'The truth is,' he continued, 'that I want to see these stars again. They are curious stars. I want to see them not from the air-ship, but from the surface of the earth, as our ancestors did, thousands of years ago. I want to visit the surface of the earth.' She was shocked again.

'Mother, you must come, if only to explain to me what is the harm of visiting the surface of the earth.'

'No harm,' she replied, controlling herself. 'But no advantage. The surface of the earth is only dust and mud, no advantage. The surface of the earth is only dust and mud, no life remains on it, and you would need a respirator, or the cold of the outer air would kill you. One dies immediately in the outer air.'

'I know; of course I shall take all precautions.'

'And besides----'

'Well?'

She considered, and chose her words with care. Her son had a queer temper, and she wished to dissuade him from the expedition.

'It is contrary to the spirit of the age,' she asserted.

'Do you mean by that, contrary to the Machine?'

'In a sense, but----'

His image is the blue plate faded.

'Kuno!'

He had isolated himself.

For a moment Vashti felt lonely.

Then she generated the light, and the sight of her room, flooded with radiance and studded with electric buttons, revived her. There were buttons and switches everywhere – buttons to call for food for music, for clothing. There was the hot-bath button, by pressure of which a basin of (imitation) marble rose out of the floor, filled to the brim with a warm deodorized liquid. There was the cold-bath button. There was the button that produced literature. And there were of course the buttons by which she communicated with her friends. The room, though it contained nothing, was in touch with all that she cared for in the world.

Vashanti's next move was to turn off the isolation switch, and all the accumulations of the last three minutes burst upon her. The room was filled with the noise of bells, and speaking-tubes. What was the new food like? Could she recommend it? Has she had any ideas lately? Might one tell her one's own ideas? Would she make an engagement to visit the public nurseries at an early date? – say this day month.

To most of these questions she replied with irritation – a growing quality in that accelerated age. She said that the new food was horrible. That she could not visit the public nurseries through press of engagements. That she had no ideas of her own but had just been told one – that four stars and three in the middle were like a man: she doubted there was much in it. Then she switched off her correspondents, for it was time to deliver her lecture on Australian music. The clumsy system of public gatherings had been long since abandoned; neither Vashti nor her audience stirred from their rooms. Seated in her armchair she spoke, while they in their armchairs heard her, fairly well, and saw her, fairly well. She opened with a humorous account of music in the pre Mongolian epoch, and went on to describe the great outburst of song that followed the Chinese conquest. Remote and primæval as were the methods of I-San-So and the Brisbane school, she yet felt (she said) that study of them might repay the musicians of today: they had freshness; they had, above all, ideas. Her lecture, which lasted ten minutes, was well received, and at its conclusion she and many of her audience listened to a lecture on the sea; there were ideas to be got from the sea; the speaker had donned a respirator and visited it lately. Then she fed, talked to many friends, had a bath, talked again, and summoned her bed. The bed was not to her liking. It was too large, and she had a feeling for a small bed.

Complaint was useless, for beds were of the same dimension all over the world, and to have had an alternative size would have involved vast alterations in the Machine. Vashti isolated herself – it was necessary, for neither day nor night existed under the ground – and reviewed all that had happened since she had summoned the bed last. Ideas? Scarcely any. Events – was Kuno's invitation an event?

By her side, on the little reading-desk, was a survival from the ages of litter – one book. This was the Book of the Machine. In it were instructions against every possible contingency. If she was hot or cold or dyspeptic or at a loss for a word, she went to the book, and it told her which button to press. The Central Committee published it. In accordance with a growing habit, it was richly bound.

Sitting up in the bed, she took it reverently in her hands. She glanced round the glowing room as if some one might be watching her. Then, half ashamed, half joyful, she murmured 'O Machine! O Machine!' and raised the volume to her lips. Thrice she kissed it, thrice inclined her head, thrice she felt the delirium of acquiescence. Her ritual performed, she turned to page 1367, which gave the times of the departure of the air-ships from the island in the southern hemisphere, under whose soil she lived, to the island in the northern hemisphere, whereunder lived her son.

She thought, 'I have not the time.'

She made the room dark and slept; she awoke and made the room light; she ate and exchanged ideas with her friends, and listened to music and attended lectures; she make the room dark and slept. Above her, beneath her, and around her, the Machine hummed eternally; she did not notice the noise, for she had been born with it in her ears. The earth, carrying her, hummed as it sped through silence, turning her now to the invisible sun, now to the invisible stars. She awoke and made the room light.

'Kuno!'

'I will not talk to you.' he answered, 'until you come.'

'Have you been on the surface of the earth since we spoke last?'

His image faded.

Again she consulted the book. She became very nervous and lay back in her chair palpitating. Think of her as without teeth or hair. Presently she directed the chair to the wall, and pressed an unfamiliar button. The wall swung apart slowly. Through the opening she saw a tunnel that curved slightly, so that its goal was not visible. Should she go to see her son, here was the beginning of the journey.

Of course she knew all about the communication-system. There was nothing mysterious in it. She would summon a car and it would fly with her down the tunnel until it reached the lift that communicated with the air-ship station: the system had been in use for many, many years, long before the universal establishment of the Machine. And of course she had studied the civilization that had immediately preceded her own – the civilization that had mistaken the functions of the system, and had used it for bringing people to things, instead of for bringing things to people. Those funny old days, when men went for change of air instead of changing the air in their rooms! And yet – she was frightened of the tunnel: she had not seen it since her last child was born. It curved – but not quite as she remembered; it was brilliant – but not quite as brilliant as a lecturer had suggested. Vashti was seized with the terrors of direct experience. She shrank back into the room, and the wall closed up again.

'Kuno,' she said, 'I cannot come to see you. I am not well.'

Immediately an enormous apparatus fell on to her out of the ceiling, a thermometer was automatically laid upon her heart. She lay powerless. Cool pads soothed her forehead. Kuno had telegraphed to her doctor.

So the human passions still blundered up and down in the Machine. Vashti drank the medicine that the doctor projected into her mouth, and the machinery retired into the ceiling. The voice of Kuno was heard asking how she felt.

'Better.' Then with irritation: 'But why do you not come to me instead?'

'Because I cannot leave this place.'

'Why?'

'Because, any moment, something tremendous may happen.'

'Have you been on the surface of the earth yet?'

'Not yet.'

'Then what is it?'

'I will not tell you through the Machine.'

She resumed her life.

But she thought of Kuno as a baby, his birth, his removal to the public nurseries, her own visit to him there, his visits to her – visits which stopped when the Machine had assigned him a room on the other side of the earth. 'Parents, duties of,' said the book of the Machine,' cease at the moment of birth. P.422327483.' True, but there was something special about Kuno – indeed there had been something special about all her children – and, after all, she must brave the journey if he desired it. And 'something tremendous might happen'. What did that mean? The nonsense of a youthful man, no doubt, but she must go. Again she pressed the unfamiliar button, again the wall swung back, and she saw the tunnel that curves out of sight. Clasping the Book, she rose, tottered on to the platform, and summoned the car. Her room closed behind her: the journey to the northern hemisphere had begun.

Of course it was perfectly easy. The car approached and in it she found armchairs exactly like her own. When she signalled, it stopped, and she tottered into the lift. One other passenger was in the lift, the first fellow creature she had seen face to face for months. Few travelled in these days, for, thanks to the advance of science, the earth was exactly alike all over. Rapid intercourse, from which the previous civilization had hoped so much, had ended by defeating itself. What was the good of going to Peking when it was just like Shrewsbury? Why return to Shrewsbury when it would all be like Peking? Men seldom moved their bodies; all unrest was concentrated in the soul.

The air-ship service was a relic from the former age. It was kept up, because it was easier to keep it up than to stop it or to diminish it, but it now far exceeded the wants of the population. Vessel after vessel would rise from the vomitories of Rye or of Christchurch (I use the antique names), would sail into the crowded sky, and would draw up at the wharves of the south – empty. So nicely adjusted was the system, so independent of meteorology, that the sky, whether calm or cloudy, resembled a vast kaleidoscope whereon the same patterns periodically recurred. The ship on which Vashti sailed started now at sunset, now at dawn. But always, as it passed above Rheas, it would neighbour the ship that served between Helsingfors and the Brazils, and, every third time it surmounted the Alps, the fleet of Palermo would cross its track behind. Night and day, wind and storm, tide and earthquake, impeded man no longer. He had harnessed Leviathan. All the old literature, with its praise of Nature, and its fear of Nature, rang false as the prattle of a child.

Yet as Vashti saw the vast flank of the ship, stained with exposure to the outer air, her horror of direct experience returned. It was not quite like the air-ship in the cinematophote. For one thing it smelt – not strongly or unpleasantly, but it did smell, and with her eyes shut she should have known that a new thing was close to her. Then she had to walk to it from the lift, had to submit to glances from the other passengers. The man in front dropped his Book – no great matter, but it disquieted them all. In the rooms, if the Book was dropped, the floor raised it mechanically, but the gangway to the air-ship was not so prepared, and the sacred volume lay motionless. They stopped – the thing was unforeseen – and the man, instead of picking up his property, felt the muscles of his arm to see how they had failed him. Then some one actually said with direct utterance: 'We shall be late' – and they trooped on board, Vashti treading on the pages as she did so.

Inside, her anxiety increased. The arrangements were old-fashioned and rough. There was even a female attendant, to whom she would have to announce her wants during the voyage. Of course a revolving platform ran the length of the boat, but she was expected to walk from it to her cabin. Some cabins were better than others, and she did not get the best. She thought the attendant had been unfair, and spasms of rage shook her. The glass valves had closed, she could not go back. She saw, at the end of the vestibule, the lift in which she had ascended going quietly up and down, empty. Beneath those corridors of shining tiles were rooms, tier below tier, reaching far into the earth, and in each room there sat a human being, eating, or sleeping, or producing ideas. And buried deep in the hive was her own room. Vashti was afraid. 'O Machine!' she murmured, and caressed her Book, and was comforted.

Then the sides of the vestibule seemed to melt together, as do the passages that we see in dreams, the lift vanished, the Book that had been dropped slid to the left and vanished, polished tiles rushed by like a stream of water, there was a slight jar, and the air-ship, issuing from its tunnel, soared above the waters of a tropical ocean.

It was night. For a moment she saw the coast of Sumatra edged by the phosphorescence of waves, and crowned by lighthouses, still sending forth their disregarded beams. These also vanished, and only the stars distracted her. They were not motionless, but swayed to and fro above her head, thronging out of one sky-light into another, as if the universe and not the air-ship was careening. And, as often happens on clear nights, they seemed now to be in perspective, now on a plane; now piled tier beyond tier into the infinite heavens, now concealing infinity, a roof limiting for ever the visions of men. In either case they seemed intolerable. 'Are we to travel in the dark?' called the passengers angrily, and the attendant, who had been careless, generated the light, and pulled down the blinds of pliable metal. When the air-ships had been built, the desire to look direct at things still lingered in the world. Hence the extraordinary number of skylights and windows, and the proportionate discomfort to those who were civilized and refined. Even in Vashti's cabin one star peeped through a flaw in the blind, and after a few hours' uneasy slumber, she was disturbed by an unfamiliar glow, which was the dawn.

Quick as the ship had sped westwards, the earth had rolled eastwards quicker still, and had dragged back Vashti and her companions towards the sun. Science could prolong the night, but only for a little, and those high hopes of neutralizing the earth's diurnal revolution had passed, together with hopes that were possibly higher. To 'keep pace with the sun,' or even to outstrip it, had been the aim of the civilization preceding this. Racing aeroplanes had been built for the purpose, capable of enormous speed, and steered by the greatest intellects of the epoch. Round the globe they went, round and round, westward, westward, round and round, amidst humanity's applause. In vain. The globe went eastward quicker still, horrible accidents occurred, and the Committee of the Machine, at the time rising into prominence, declared the pursuit illegal, unmechanical, and punishable by Homelessness.

Of Homelessness more will be said later.

Doubtless the Committee was right. Yet the attempt to 'defeat the sun' aroused the last common interest that our race experienced about the heavenly bodies, or indeed about anything. It was the last time that men were compacted by thinking of a power outside the world. The sun had conquered, yet it was the end of his spiritual dominion. Dawn, midday, twilight, the zodiacal path, touched neither men's lives not their hearts, and science retreated into the ground, to concentrate herself upon problems that she was certain of solving.

So when Vashti found her cabin invaded by a rosy finger of light, she was annoyed, and tried to adjust the blind. But the blind flew up altogether, and she saw through the skylight small pink clouds, swaying against a background of blue, and as the sun crept higher, its radiance entered direct, brimming down the wall, like a golden sea. It rose and fell with the air-ship's motion, just as waves rise and fall, but it advanced steadily, as a tide advances. Unless she was careful, it would strike her face. A spasm of horror shook her and she rang for the attendant. The attendant too was horrified, but she could do nothing; it was not her place to mend the blind. She could only suggest that the lady should change her cabin, which she accordingly prepared to do.

People were almost exactly alike all over the world, but the attendant of the air-ship, perhaps owing to her exceptional duties, had grown a little out of the common. She had often to address passengers with direct speech, and this had given her a certain roughness and originality of manner. When Vashti swerved away from the sunbeams with a cry, she behaved barbarically – she put out her hand to steady her.

'How dare you!' exclaimed the passenger. 'You forget

yourself!'

The woman was confused, and apologized for not having let her fall. People never touched one another. The custom had become obsolete, owing to the Machine.

'Where are we now?' asked Vashti haughtily.

'We are over Asia,' said the attendant, anxious to be polite.

'Asia?'

'You must excuse my common way of speaking. I have got into the habit of calling places over which I pass by their unmechanical names.'

'Oh, I remember Asia. The Mongols came from it.'

'Beneath us, in the open air, stood a city that was once called Simla.' 'Have you ever heard of the Mongols and of the Brisbane school?'

'No.'

'Brisbane also stood in the open air.'

'Those mountains to the right – let me show you them.' She pushed back a metal blind. The main chain of the Himalayas was revealed. 'They were once called the Roof of the World, those mountains.'

'You must remember that, before the dawn of civilization, they seemed to be an impenetrable wall that touched the stars. It was supposed that no one but the gods could exist above their summits. How we have advanced, thanks to the Machine!'

'How we have advanced, thanks to the Machine!' said Vashti.

'How we have advanced, thanks to the Machine!' echoed the passenger who had dropped his Book the night before, and who was standing in the passage.

'And that white stuff in the cracks? – what is it?'

'I have forgotten its name.'

'Cover the window, please. These mountains give me no ideas.'

The northern aspect of the Himalayas was in deep shadow: on the Indian slope the sun had just prevailed. The forests had been destroyed during the literature epoch for the purpose of making newspaper-pulp, but the snows were awakening to their morning glory, and clouds still hung on the breasts of Kinchinjunga. In the plain were seen the ruins of cities, with diminished rivers creeping by their walls, and by the sides of these were sometimes the signs of vomitories, marking the cities of today. Over the whole prospect air-ships rushed, crossing the inter-crossing with incredible *aplomb*, and rising nonchalantly when they desired to escape the perturbations of the lower atmosphere and to traverse the Roof of the World.

'We have indeed advanced, thanks to the Machine,' repeated the attendant, and hid the Himalayas behind a metal blind.

The day dragged wearily forward. The passengers sat each in his cabin, avoiding one another with an almost physical repulsion and longing to be once more under the surface of the earth. There were eight or ten of them, mostly young males, sent out from the public nurseries to inhabit the rooms of those who had died in various parts of the earth. The man who had dropped his Book was on the homeward journey. He had been sent to Sumatra for the purpose of propagating the race. Vashti alone was travelling by her private will.

At midday she took a second glance at the earth. The air-ship was crossing another range of mountains, but she could see little, owing to clouds. Masses of black rock hovered below her, and merged indistinctly into grey. Their shapes were fantastic; one of them resembled a prostrate man.

'No ideas here,' murmured Vashti, and hid the Caucasus behind a metal blind. In the evening she looked again. They were crossing a golden sea, in which lay many small islands and one peninsula. She repeated, 'No ideas here,' and hid Greece behind a metal blind.

THE MENDING APPARATUS

BY a vestibule, by a lift, by a tubular railway, by a platform, by a sliding door – by reversing all the steps of her departure did Vashti arrive at her son's room, which exactly resembled her own. She might well declare that the visit was superfluous. The buttons, the knobs, the reading-desk with the Book, the temperature, the atmosphere, the illumination – all were exactly the same. And if Kuno himself, flesh of her flesh, stood close beside her at last, what profit was there in that? She was too well-bred to shake him by the hand. Averting her eyes, she spoke as follows:

'Here I am. I have had the most terrible journey and greatly retarded the development of my soul. It is not worth it, Kuno, it is not worth it. My time is too precious. The sunlight almost touched me, and I have met with the rudest people. I can only stop a few minutes. Say what you want to say, and then I must return.'

'I have been threatened with Homelessness,' said Kuno. She looked at him now.

'I have been threatened with Homelessness, and I could not tell you such a thing through the Machine.' Homelessness means death. The victim is exposed to the air, which kills him.

'I have been outside since I spoke to you last. The tremendous thing has happened, and they have discovered me.'

'But why shouldn't you go outside?' she exclaimed, 'It is perfectly legal, perfectly mechanical, to visit the surface of the earth. I have lately been to a lecture on the sea; there is no objection to that; one simply summons a respirator and gets an Egression-permit. It is not the kind of thing that spiritually minded people do, and I begged you not to do it, but there is no legal objection to it.'

'I did not get an Egression-permit.'

'Then how did you get out?'

'I found out a way of my own.' The phrase conveyed no meaning to her, and he had to repeat it.

'A way of your own?' she whispered. 'But that would be wrong.'

'Why?'

The question shocked her beyond measure.

'You are beginning to worship the Machine,' he said coldly. 'You think it irreligious of me to have found out a way of my own. It was just what the Committee thought, when they threatened me with Homelessness.'

At this she grew angry. 'I worship nothing!' she cried. 'I am most advanced. I don't think you irreligious, for there is no such thing as religion left. All the fear and the superstition that existed once have been destroyed by the Machine. I only meant that to find out a way of your own was----Besides, there is no new way out.'

'So it is always supposed.'

'Except through the vomitories, for which one must have an Egression-permit, it is impossible to get out. The Book says so.'

'Well, the Book's wrong, for I have been out on my feet.'

For Kuno was possessed of a certain physical strength.

By these days it was a demerit to be muscular. Each infant was examined at birth, and all who promised undue strength were destroyed. Humanitarians may protest, but it would have been no true kindness to let an athlete live; he would never have been happy in that state of life to which the Machine had called him; he would have yearned for trees to climb, rivers to bathe in, meadows and hills against which he might measure his body. Man must be adapted to his surroundings, must he not? In the dawn of the world our weakly must be exposed on Mount Taygetus, in its twilight our strong will suffer euthanasia, that the Machine may progress, that the Machine may progress, that the Machine may progress eternally.

'You know that we have lost the sense of space. We say 'space is annihilated', but we have annihilated not space, but the sense thereof. We have lost a part of ourselves. I determined to recover it, and I began by walking up and down the platform of the railway outside my room. Up and down, until I was tired, and so did recapture the meaning of "Near" and "Far". "Near" is a place to which I can get quickly on my feet, not a place to which the train or the air-ship will take me quickly. 'Far' is a place to which I cannot get quickly on my feet; the vomitory is 'far', though I could be there in thirty-eight seconds by summoning the train. Man is the measure. That was my first lesson. Man's feet are the measure for distance, his hands are the measure for ownership, his body is the measure for all that is lovable and desirable and strong. Then I went further: it was then that I called to you for the first time, and you would not come.

'This city, as you know, is built deep beneath the surface of the earth, with only the vomitories protruding. Having paced the platform outside my own room, I took the lift to the next platform and paced that also, and so with each in turn, until I came to the topmost, above which begins the earth. All the platforms were exactly alike, and all that I gained by visiting them was to develop my sense of space and my muscles. I think I should have been content with this – it is not a little thing, – but as I walked and brooded, it occurred to me that our cities had been built in the days when men still breathed the outer air, and that there had been ventilation shafts for the workmen. I could think of nothing but these ventilation shafts. Had they been destroyed by all the food-tubes and medicine-tubes and music-tubes that the Machine has evolved lately? Or did traces of them remain? One thing was certain. If I came upon them anywhere, it would be in the railway-tunnels of the topmost storey. Everywhere else, all space was accounted for.

'I am telling my story quickly, but don't think that I was not a coward or that your answers never depressed me. It is not the proper thing, it is not mechanical, it is not decent to walk along a railway-tunnel. I did not fear that I might tread upon a live rail and be killed. I feared something far more intangible – doing what was not contemplated by the Machine. Then I said to myself, "Man is the measure", and I went, and after many visits I found an opening.

'The tunnels, of course, were lighted. Everything is light, artificial light; darkness is the exception. So when I saw a black gap in the tiles, I knew that it was an exception, and rejoiced. I put in my arm – I could put in no more at first – and waved it round and round in ecstasy. I loosened another tile, and put in my head, and shouted into the darkness: "I am coming, I shall do it yet," and my voice reverberated down endless passages. I seemed to hear the spirits of those dead workmen who had returned each evening to the starlight and to their wives, and all the generations who had lived in the open air called back to me, "You will do it yet, you are coming,"'

He paused, and, absurd as he was, his last words moved her.

For Kuno had lately asked to be a father, and his request had been refused by the Committee. His was not a type that the Machine desired to hand on.

'Then a train passed. It brushed by me, but I thrust my head and arms into the hole. I had done enough for one day, so I crawled back to the platform, went down in the lift, and summoned my bed. Ah what dreams! And again I called you, and again you refused.'

She shook her head and said:

'Don't. Don't talk of these terrible things. You make me miserable. You are throwing civilization away.'

'But I had got back the sense of space and a man cannot rest then. I determined to get in at the hole and climb the shaft. And so I exercised my arms. Day after day I went through ridiculous movements, until my flesh ached, and I could hang by my hands and hold the pillow of my bed outstretched for many minutes. Then I summoned a respirator, and started.

'It was easy at first. The mortar had somehow rotted, and I soon pushed some more tiles in, and clambered after them into the darkness, and the spirits of the dead comforted me. I don't know what I mean by that. I just say what I felt. I felt, for the first time, that a protest had been lodged against corruption, and that even as the dead were comforting me, so I was comforting the unborn. I felt that humanity existed, and that it existed without clothes. How can I possibly explain this? It was naked, humanity seemed naked, and all these tubes and buttons and machineries neither came into the world with us, nor will they follow us out, nor do they matter supremely while we are here. Had I been strong, I would have torn off every garment I had, and gone out into the outer air unswaddled. But this is not for me, nor perhaps for my generation. I climbed with my respirator and my hygienic clothes and my dietetic tabloids! Better thus than not at all.

'There was a ladder, made of some primæval metal. The light from the railway fell upon its lowest rungs, and I saw that it led straight upwards out of the rubble at the bottom of the shaft. Perhaps our ancestors ran up and down it a dozen times daily, in their building. As I climbed, the rough edges cut through my gloves so that my hands bled. The light helped me for a little, and then came darkness and, worse still, silence which pierced my ears like a sword. The Machine hums! Did you know that? Its hum penetrates our blood, and may even guide our thoughts. Who knows! I was getting beyond its power. Then I thought: 'This silence means that I am doing wrong.' But I heard voices in the silence, and again they strengthened me.' He laughed. 'I had need of them. The next moment I cracked my head against something.' She sighed. 'I had reached one of those pneumatic stoppers that defend us from the outer air. You may have noticed them on the air-ship. Pitch dark, my feet on the rungs of an invisible ladder, my hands cut; I cannot explain how I lived through this part, but the voices still comforted me, and I felt for fastenings. The stopper, I suppose, was about eight feet across. I passed my hand over it as far as I could reach. It was perfectly smooth. I felt it almost to the centre. Not quite to the centre, for my arm was too short. Then the voice said: "Jump. It is worth it. There may be a handle in the centre, and you may catch hold of it and so come to us your own way. And if there is no handle, so that you may fall and are dashed to – it is still worth it: you will still come to us your own way." So I jumped. There was a handle, and ----'

He paused. Tears gathered in his mother's eyes. She knew that he was fated. If he did not die today he would die tomorrow. There was not room for such a person in the world. And with her pity disgust mingled. She was ashamed at having borne such a son, she who had always been so respectable and so full of ideas. Was he really the little boy to whom she had taught the use of his stops and buttons, and to whom she had given his first lessons in the Book? The very hair that disfigured his lip showed that he was reverting to some savage type. On atavism the Machine can have no mercy.

'There was a handle, and I did catch it. I hung tranced over the darkness and heard the hum of these workings as the last whisper in a dying dream. All the things I had cared about and all the people I had spoken to through tubes appeared infinitely little. Meanwhile the handle revolved. My weight had set something in motion and I span slowly, and then----

'I cannot describe it. I was lying with my face to the sunshine. Blood poured from my nose and ears and I heard a tremendous roaring. The stopper, with me clinging to it, had simply been blown out of the earth, and the air that we make down here was escaping through the vent into the air above. It burst up like a fountain. I crawled back to it – for the upper air hurts – and, as it were, I took great sips from the edge. My respirator had flown goodness knows where, my clothes were torn. I just lay with my lips close to the hole, and I sipped until the bleeding stopped. You can imagine nothing so curious. This hollow in the grass – I will speak of it in a minute, – the sun shining into it, not brilliantly but through marbled clouds, – the peace, the nonchalance, the sense of space, and, brushing my cheek, the roaring fountain of our artificial air! Soon I spied my respirator, bobbing up and down in the current high above my head, and higher still were many air-ships. But no one ever looks out of air-ships, and in any case they could not have picked me up. There I was, stranded. The sun shone a little way down the shaft, and revealed the topmost rung of the ladder, but it was hopeless trying to reach it. I should either have been tossed up again by the escape, or else have fallen in, and died. I could only lie on the grass, sipping and sipping, and from time to time glancing around me.

'I knew that I was in Wessex, for I had taken care to go to a lecture on the subject before starting. Wessex lies above the room in which we are talking now. It was once an important state. Its kings held all the southern coast from the Andredswald to Cornwall, while the Wansdyke protected them on the north, running over the high ground. The lecturer was only concerned with the rise of Wessex, so I do not know how long it remained an international power, nor would the knowledge have assisted me. To tell the truth I could do nothing but laugh, during this part. There was I, with a pneumatic stopper by my side and a respirator bobbing over my head, imprisoned, all three of us, in a grass-grown hollow that was edged with fern.' Then he grew grave again.

'Lucky for me that it was a hollow. For the air began to fall back into it and to fill it as water fills a bowl. I could crawl about. Presently I stood. I breathed a mixture, in which the air that hurts predominated whenever I tried to climb the sides. This was not so bad. I had not lost my tabloids and remained ridiculously cheerful, and as for the Machine, I forgot about it altogether. My one aim now was to get to the top, where the ferns were, and to view whatever objects lay beyond.

'I rushed the slope. The new air was still too bitter for me and I came rolling back, after a momentary vision of something grey. The sun grew very feeble, and I remembered that he was in Scorpio – I had been to a lecture on that too. If the sun is in Scorpio, and you are in Wessex, it means that you must be as quick as you can, or it will get too dark. (This is the first bit of useful information I have ever got from a lecture, and I expect it will be the last.) It made me try frantically to breathe the new air, and to advance as far as I dared out of my pond. The hollow filled so slowly. At times I thought that the fountain played with less vigour. My respirator seemed to dance nearer the earth; the roar was decreasing.' He broke off.

'I don't think this is interesting you. The rest will interest you even less. There are no ideas in it, and I wish that I had not troubled you to come. We are too different, mother.' She told him to continue.

'It was evening before I climbed the bank. The sun had very nearly slipped out of the sky by this time, and I could not get a good view. You, who have just crossed the Roof of the World, will not want to hear an account of the little hills that I saw – low colourless hills. But to me they were living and the turf that covered them was a skin, under which their muscles rippled, and I felt that those hills had called with incalculable force to men in the past, and that men had loved them. Now they sleep – perhaps for ever. They commune with humanity in dreams. Happy the man, happy the woman, who awakes the hills of Wessex. For though they sleep, they will never die.'

His voice rose passionately.

'Cannot you see, cannot all you lecturers see, that it is we that are dying, and that down here the only thing that really lives is the Machine? We created the Machine, to do our will, but we cannot make it do our will now. It has robbed us of the sense of space and of the sense of touch, it has blurred every human relation and narrowed down love to a carnal act, it has paralysed our bodies and our wills, and now it compels us to worship it. The Machine develops – but not on our lines. The Machine proceeds – but not to our goal. We only exist as the blood corpuscles that course through its arteries, and if it could work without us, it would let us die. Oh, I have no remedy – or, at least, only one – to tell men again and again that I have seen the hills of Wessex as Ælfrid saw them when he overthrew the Danes.

'So the sun set. I forgot to mention that a belt of mist lay between my hill and other hills, and that it was the colour of pearl.' He broke off for the second time.

'Go on,' said his mother wearily. He shook his head.

'Go on. Nothing that you say can distress me now. I am hardened.'

'I had meant to tell you the rest, but I cannot: I know that I cannot: good-bye.' Vashti stood irresolute. All her nerves were tingling with his blasphemies. But she was also inquisitive.

'This is unfair,' she complained. 'You have called me across the world to hear your story, and hear it I will. Tell me – as briefly as possible, for this is a disastrous waste of time – tell me how you returned to civilization.'

'Oh – that!' he said, starting. 'You would like to hear about civilization. Certainly. Had I got to where my respirator fell down?'

'No – but I understand everything now. You put on your respirator, and managed to walk along the surface of the earth to a vomitory, and there your conduct was reported to the Central Committee.'

'By no means.'

He passed his hand over his forehead, as if dispelling some strong impression. Then, resuming his narrative, he warmed to it again.

'My respirator fell about sunset. I had mentioned that the fountain seemed feebler, had I not?'

'Yes.'

'About sunset, it let the respirator fall. As I said, I had entirely forgotten about the Machine, and I paid no great attention at the time, being occupied with other things. I had my pool of air, into which I could dip when the outer keenness became intolerable, and which would possibly remain for days, provided that no wind sprang up to disperse it. Not until it was too late did I realize what the stoppage of the escape implied. You see – the gap in the tunnel had been mended; the Mending Apparatus; the Mending Apparatus, was after me.

'One other warning I had, but I neglected it. The sky at night was clearer than it had been in the day, and the moon, which was about half the sky behind the sun, shone into the dell at moments quite brightly. I was in my usual place – on the boundary between the two atmospheres – when I thought I saw something dark move across the bottom of the dell, and vanish into the shaft. In my folly, I ran down. I bent over and listened, and I thought I heard a faint scraping noise in the depths.

'At this – but it was too late – I took alarm. I determined to put on my respirator and to walk right out of the dell. But my respirator had gone. I knew exactly where it had fallen – between the stopper and the aperture – and I could even feel the mark that it had made in the turf. It had gone, and I realized that something evil was at work, and I had better escape to the other air, and, if I must die, die running towards the cloud that had been the colour of a pearl. I never started. Out of the shaft – it is too horrible. A worm, a long white worm, had crawled out of the shaft and was gliding over the moonlit grass.

'I screamed. I did everything that I should not have done, I stamped upon the creature instead of flying from it, and it at once curled round the ankle. Then we fought. The worm let me run all over the dell, but edged up my leg as I ran. 'Help!' I cried. (That part is too awful. It belongs to the part that you will never know.) 'Help!' I cried. (Why cannot we suffer in silence?) 'Help!' I cried. When my feet were wound together, I fell, I was dragged away from the dear ferns and the living hills, and past the great metal stopper (I can tell you this part), and I thought it might save me again if I caught hold of the handle. It also was enwrapped, it also. Oh, the whole dell was full of the things. They were searching it in all directions, they were denuding it, and the white snouts of others peeped out of the hole, ready if needed.

Everything that could be moved they brought – brushwood, bundles of fern, everything, and down we all went intertwined into hell. The last things that I saw, ere the stopper closed after us, were certain stars, and I felt that a man of my sort lived in the sky. For I did fight, I fought till the very end, and it was only my head hitting against the ladder that quieted me. I woke up in this room. The worms had vanished. I was surrounded by artificial air, artificial light, artificial peace, and my friends were calling to me down speaking-tubes to know whether I had come across any new ideas lately.'

Here his story ended. Discussion of it was impossible, and Vashti turned to go.

'It will end in Homelessness,' she said quietly.

'I wish it would,' retorted Kuno.

'The Machine has been most merciful.'

'I prefer the mercy of God.'

'By that superstitious phrase, do you mean that you could live in the outer air?'

'Yes.'

'Have you ever seen, round the vomitories, the bones of those who were extruded after the Great Rebellion?'

'Yes.'

'They were left where they perished for our edification. A few crawled away, but they perished, too – who can doubt it? And so with the Homeless of our own day. The surface of the earth supports life no longer.'

'Indeed.'

'Ferns and a little grass may survive, but all higher forms have perished. Has any air-ship detected them?'

'No.'

'Has any lecturer dealt with them?'

'No.'

'Then why this obstinacy?'

'Because I have seen them,' he exploded.

'Seen what?'

'Because I have seen her in the twilight – because she came to my help when I called – because she, too, was entangled by the worms, and, luckier than I, was killed by one of them piercing her throat.'

He was mad. Vashti departed, nor, in the troubles that followed, did she ever see his face again.

THE HOMELESS

DURING the years that followed Kuno's escapade, two important developments took place in the Machine. On the surface they were revolutionary, but in either case men's minds had been prepared beforehand, and they did but express tendencies that were latent already. The first of these was the abolition of respirators.

Advanced thinkers, like Vashti, had always held it foolish to visit the surface of the earth. Air-ships might be necessary, but what was the good of going out for mere curiosity and crawling along for a mile or two in a terrestrial motor? The habit was vulgar and perhaps faintly improper: it was unproductive of ideas, and had no connection with the habits that really mattered. So respirators were abolished, and with them, of course, the terrestrial motors, and except for a few lecturers, who complained that they were debarred access to their subject- matter, the development was accepted quietly. Those who still wanted to know what the earth was like had after all only to listen to some gramophone, or to look into some cinematophote. And even the lecturers acquiesced when they found that a lecture on the sea was none the less stimulating when compiled out of other lectures that had already been delivered on the same subject. 'Beware of first-hand ideas!' exclaimed one of the most advanced of them. 'First-hand ideas do not really exist. They are but the physical impressions produced by love and fear, and on this gross foundation who could erect a philosophy? Let your ideas be second-hand, and if possible tenth-hand, for then they will be far removed from that disturbing element – direct observation. Do not learn anything about this subject of mine – the French Revolution. Learn instead what I think that Enicharmon thought Urizen thought Gutch thought Ho-

Yung thought Chi-Bo-Sing thought Lafcadio Hearn thought Carlyle thought Mirabeau said about the French Revolution.

Through the medium of these eight great minds, the blood that was shed at Paris and the windows that were broken at Versailles will be clarified to an idea which you may employ most profitably in your daily lives. But be sure that the intermediates are many and varied, for in history one authority exists to counteract another. Urizen must counteract the scepticism of Ho-Yung and Enicharmon, I must myself counteract the impetuosity of Gutch. You who listen to me are in a better position to judge about the French Revolution than I am. Your descendants will be even in a better position than you, for they will learn what you think I think, and yet another intermediate will be added to the chain. And in time' – his voice rose – 'there will come a generation that had got beyond facts, beyond impressions, a generation absolutely colourless, a generation

'seraphically free
from taint of personality,'

which will see the French Revolution not as it happened, nor as they would like it to have happened, but as it would have happened, had it taken place in the days of the Machine.'

Tremendous applause greeted this lecture, which did but voice a feeling already latent in the minds of men – a feeling that terrestrial facts must be ignored, and that the abolition of respirators was a positive gain. It was even suggested that air-ships should be abolished too. This was not done, because air-ships had somehow worked themselves into the Machine's system. But year by year they were used less, and mentioned less by thoughtful men.

The second great development was the re-establishment of religion.

This, too, had been voiced in the celebrated lecture. No one could mistake the reverent tone in which the peroration had concluded, and it awakened a responsive echo in the heart of each. Those who had long worshipped silently, now began to talk. They described the strange feeling of peace that came over them when they handled the Book of the Machine, the pleasure that it was to repeat certain numerals out of it, however little meaning those numerals conveyed to the outward ear, the ecstasy of touching a button, however unimportant, or of ringing an electric bell, however superfluously.

'The Machine,' they exclaimed, 'feeds us and clothes us and houses us; through it we speak to one another, through it we see one another, in it we have our being. The Machine is the friend of ideas and the enemy of superstition: the Machine is omnipotent, eternal; blessed is the Machine.' And before long this allocution was printed on the first page of the Book, and in subsequent editions the ritual swelled into a complicated system of praise and prayer. The word 'religion' was sedulously avoided, and in theory the Machine was still the creation and the implement of man. But in practice all, save a few retrogrades, worshipped it as divine. Nor was it worshipped in unity. One believer would be chiefly impressed by the blue optic plates, through which he saw other believers; another by the mending apparatus, which sinful Kuno had compared to worms; another by the lifts, another by the Book. And each would pray to this or to that, and ask it to intercede for him with the Machine as a whole. Persecution – that also was present. It did not break out, for reasons that will be set forward shortly. But it was latent, and all who did not accept the minimum known as 'undenominational Mechanism' lived in danger of Homelessness, which means death, as we know.

To attribute these two great developments to the Central Committee, is to take a very narrow view of civilization. The Central Committee announced the developments, it is true, but they were no more the cause of them than were the kings of the imperialistic period the cause of war. Rather did they yield to some invincible pressure, which came no one knew whither, and which, when gratified, was succeeded by some new pressure equally invincible. To such a state of affairs it is convenient to give the name of progress. No one confessed the

Machine was out of hand. Year by year it was served with increased efficiency and decreased intelligence. The better a man knew his own duties upon it, the less he understood the duties of his neighbour, and in all the world there was not one who understood the monster as a whole. Those master brains had perished. They had left full directions, it is true, and their successors had each of them mastered a portion of those directions. But Humanity, in its desire for comfort, had over-reached itself. It had exploited the riches of nature too far. Quietly and complacently, it was sinking into decadence, and progress had come to mean the progress of the Machine.

As for Vashti, her life went peacefully forward until the final disaster. She made her room dark and slept; she awoke and made the room light. She lectured and attended lectures. She exchanged ideas with her innumerable friends and believed she was growing more spiritual. At times a friend was granted Euthanasia, and left his or her room for the homelessness that is beyond all human conception. Vashti did not much mind. After an unsuccessful lecture, she would sometimes ask for Euthanasia herself. But the death-rate was not permitted to exceed the birth-rate, and the Machine had hitherto refused it to her.

The troubles began quietly, long before she was conscious of them.

One day she was astonished at receiving a message from her son. They never communicated, having nothing in common, and she had only heard indirectly that he was still alive, and had been transferred from the northern hemisphere, where he had behaved so mischievously, to the southern – indeed, to a room not far from her own.

'Does he want me to visit him?' she thought. 'Never again, never. And I have not the time.' No, it was madness of another kind.

He refused to visualize his face upon the blue plate, and speaking out of the darkness with solemnity said: 'The Machine stops.'

'What do you say?'

'The Machine is stopping, I know it, I know the signs.' She burst into a peal of laughter. He heard her and was angry, and they spoke no more. 'Can you imagine anything more absurd?' she cried to a friend. 'A man who was my son believes that the Machine is stopping. It would be impious if it was not mad.'

'The Machine is stopping?' her friend replied. 'What does that mean? The phrase conveys nothing to me.'

'Nor to me.'

'He does not refer, I suppose, to the trouble there has been lately with the music?'

'Oh no, of course not. Let us talk about music.'

'Have you complained to the authorities?'

'Yes, and they say it wants mending, and referred me to the Committee of the Mending Apparatus. I complained of those curious gasping sighs that disfigure the symphonies of the Brisbane school. They sound like some one in pain. The Committee of the Mending Apparatus say that it shall be remedied shortly.'

Obscurely worried, she resumed her life. For one thing, the defect in the music irritated her. For another thing, she could not forget Kuno's speech. If he had known that the music was out of repair – he could not know it, for he detested music – if he had known that it was wrong, 'the Machine stops' was exactly the venomous sort of remark he would have made. Of course he had made it at a venture, but the coincidence annoyed her, and she spoke with some petulance to the Committee of the Mending Apparatus.

They replied, as before, that the defect would be set right shortly.

'Shortly! At once!' she retorted. 'Why should I be worried by imperfect music? Things are always put right at once. If you do not mend it at once, I shall complain to the Central Committee.' 'No personal complaints are received by the Central Committee,' the Committee of the Mending Apparatus replied.

'Through whom am I to make my complaint, then?'

'Through us.'

'I complain then.'

'Your complaint shall be forwarded in its turn.'

'Have others complained?' This question was unmechanical, and the Committee of the Mending Apparatus refused to answer it.

'It is too bad!' she exclaimed to another of her friends.

'There never was such an unfortunate woman as myself. I can never be sure of my music now. It gets worse and worse each time I summon it.'

'I too have my troubles,' the friend replied. "Sometimes my ideas are interrupted by a slight jarring noise.'

'What is it?'

'I do not know whether it is inside my head, or inside the wall.'

'Complain, in either case.'

'I have complained, and my complaint will be forwarded in its turn to the Central Committee.' Time passed, and they resented the defects no longer. The defects had not been remedied, but the human tissues in that latter day had become so subservient, that they readily adapted themselves to every caprice of the Machine. The sigh at the crises of the Brisbane symphony no longer irritated Vashti; she accepted it as part of the melody. The jarring noise, whether in the head or in the wall, was no longer resented by her friend. And so with the mouldy artificial fruit, so with the bath water that began to stink, so with the defective rhymes that the poetry machine had taken to emit. All were bitterly complained of at first, and then acquiesced in and forgotten. Things went from bad to worse unchallenged.

It was otherwise with the failure of the sleeping apparatus. That was a more serious stoppage. There came a day when over the whole world – in Sumatra, in Wessex, in the innumerable cities of Courland and Brazil – the beds, when summoned by their tired owners, failed to appear. It may seem a ludicrous matter, but from it we may date the collapse of humanity. The Committee responsible for the failure was assailed by complainants, whom it referred, as usual, to the Committee of the Mending Apparatus, who in its turn assured them that their complaints would be forwarded to the Central Committee. But the discontent grew, for mankind was not yet sufficiently adaptable to do without sleeping.

'Some one is meddling with the Machine---' they began.

'Some one is trying to make himself king, to reintroduce the personal element.'

'Punish that man with Homelessness.'

'To the rescue! Avenge the Machine! Avenge the Machine!'

'War! Kill the man!'

But the Committee of the Mending Apparatus now came forward, and allayed the panic with well-chosen words. It confessed that the Mending Apparatus was itself in need of repair.

The effect of this frank confession was admirable.

'Of course,' said a famous lecturer – he of the French Revolution, who gilded each new decay with splendour – 'of course we shall not press our complaints now. The Mending Apparatus has treated us so well in the past that we all sympathize with it, and will wait patiently for its recovery. In its own good time it will resume its duties. Meanwhile let us do without our beds, our tabloids, our other little wants. Such, I feel sure, would be the wish of the Machine.' Thousands of miles away his audience applauded. The Machine still linked them. Under the seas, beneath the roots of the mountains, ran the wires through which they saw and heard, the enormous eyes and ears that were their heritage, and the hum of many workings clothed their thoughts in one garment of subserviency. Only the old and the sick remained ungrateful, for it was rumoured that Euthanasia, too, was out of order, and that pain had reappeared among men.

It became difficult to read. A blight entered the atmosphere and dulled its luminosity. At times Vashti could scarcely see across her room. The air, too, was foul. Loud were the complaints, impotent the remedies, heroic the tone of the lecturer as he cried: 'Courage! courage! What matter so long as the Machine goes on? To it the darkness and the light are one.' And though things improved again after a time, the old brilliancy was never recaptured, and humanity never recovered from its entrance into twilight. There was an hysterical talk of 'measures,' of 'provisional dictatorship,' and the inhabitants of Sumatra were asked to familiarize themselves with the workings of the central power station, the said power station being situated in France. But for the most part panic reigned, and men spent their strength praying to their Books, tangible proofs of the Machine's omnipotence. There were gradations of terror – at times came rumours of hope-the Mending Apparatus was almost mended – the enemies of the Machine had been got under – new 'nerve-centres' were evolving which would do the work even more magnificently than before. But there came a day when, without the slightest warning, without any previous hint of feebleness, the entire communication-system broke down, all over the world, and the world, as they understood it, ended.

Vashti was lecturing at the time and her earlier remarks had been punctuated with applause. As she proceeded the audience became silent, and at the conclusion there was no sound. Somewhat displeased, she called to a friend who was a specialist in sympathy. No sound: doubtless the friend was sleeping. And so with the next friend whom she tried to summon, and so with the next, until she remembered Kuno's cryptic remark, 'The Machine stops'.

The phrase still conveyed nothing. If Eternity was stopping it would of course be set going shortly.

For example, there was still a little light and air – the atmosphere had improved a few hours previously. There was still the Book, and while there was the Book there was security.

Then she broke down, for with the cessation of activity came an unexpected terror – silence. She had never known silence, and the coming of it nearly killed her – it did kill many thousands of people outright. Ever since her birth she had been surrounded by the steady hum. It was to the ear what artificial air was to the lungs, and agonizing pains shot across her head. And scarcely knowing what she did, she stumbled forward and pressed the unfamiliar button, the one that opened the door of her cell.

Now the door of the cell worked on a simple hinge of its own. It was not connected with the central power station, dying far away in France. It opened, rousing immoderate hopes in Vashti, for she thought that the Machine had been mended. It opened, and she saw the dim tunnel that curved far away towards freedom. One look, and then she shrank back. For the tunnel was full of people – she was almost the last in that city to have taken alarm.

People at any time repelled her, and these were nightmares from her worst dreams. People were crawling about, people were screaming, whimpering, gasping for breath, touching each other, vanishing in the dark, and ever and anon being pushed off the platform on to the live rail. Some were fighting round the electric bells, trying to summon trains which could not be summoned.

Others were yelling for Euthanasia or for respirators, or blaspheming the Machine. Others stood at the doors of their cells fearing, like herself, either to stop in them or to leave them. And behind all the uproar was silence – the silence which is the voice of the earth and of the generations who have gone.

No – it was worse than solitude. She closed the door again and sat down to wait for the end. The disintegration went on, accompanied by horrible cracks and rumbling. The valves that restrained the Medical Apparatus must have weakened, for it ruptured and hung hideously from the ceiling. The floor heaved and fell and flung her from the chair. A tube oozed towards her serpent fashion. And at last the final horror approached – light began to ebb, and she knew that civilization's long day was closing.

She whirled around, praying to be saved from this, at any rate, kissing the Book, pressing button after button. The uproar outside was increasing, and even penetrated the wall. Slowly the brilliancy of her cell was dimmed, the reflections faded from the metal switches. Now she could not see the reading-stand, now not the Book, though she held it in her hand. Light followed the flight of sound, air was following light, and the original void returned to the cavern from which it has so long been excluded. Vashti continued to whirl, like the devotees of an earlier religion, screaming, praying, striking at the buttons with bleeding hands. It was thus that she opened her prison and escaped – escaped in the spirit: at least so it seems to me, ere my meditation closes. That she escapes in the body – I cannot perceive that. She struck, by chance, the switch that released the door, and the rush of foul air on her skin, the loud throbbing whispers in her ears, told her that she was facing the tunnel again, and that tremendous platform on which she had seen men fighting. They were not fighting now. Only the whispers remained, and the little whimpering groans. They were dying by hundreds out in the dark.

She burst into tears.

Tears answered her.

They wept for humanity, those two, not for themselves. They could not bear that this should be the end. Ere silence was completed their hearts were opened, and they knew what had been important on the earth. Man, the flower of all flesh, the noblest of all creatures visible, man who had once made god in his image, and had mirrored his strength on the constellations, beautiful naked man was dying, strangled in the garments that he had woven. Century after century had he toiled, and here was his reward. Truly the garment had seemed heavenly at first, shot with colours of culture, sewn with the threads of self-denial. And heavenly it had been so long as man could shed it at will and live by the essence that is his soul, and the essence, equally divine, that is his body. The sin against the body – it was for that they wept in chief; the centuries of wrong against the muscles and the nerves, and those five portals by which we can alone apprehend – glozing it over with talk of evolution, until the body was white pap, the home of ideas as colourless, last sloshy stirrings of a spirit that had grasped the stars.

'Where are you?' she sobbed.

His voice in the darkness said, 'Here.'

'Is there any hope, Kuno?'

'None for us.'

'Where are you?' She crawled towards him over the bodies of the dead. His blood spurted over her hands.

'Quicker,' he gasped, 'I am dying – but we touch, we talk, not through the Machine.' He kissed her.

'We have come back to our own. We die, but we have recaptured life, as it was in Wessex, when Ælfrid overthrew the Danes. We know what they know outside, they who dwelt in the cloud that is the colour of a pearl.'

'But Kuno, is it true? Are there still men on the surface of the earth? Is this – tunnel, this poisoned darkness – really not the end?'

He replied: 'I have seen them, spoken to them, loved them. They are hiding in the mist and the ferns until our civilization stops. Today they are the Homeless – tomorrow----- '

'Oh, tomorrow – some fool will start the Machine again, tomorrow.'

'Never,' said Kuno, 'never. Humanity has learnt its lesson.'

As he spoke, the whole city was broken like a honeycomb. An air-ship had sailed in through the vomitory into a ruined wharf. It crashed downwards, exploding as it went, rending gallery after gallery with its wings of steel. For a moment they saw the nations of the dead, and, before they joined them, scraps of the untainted sky.

THE END

HISTORICAL CONTEXT

During the period this book was originally written, the world was a very different place. The events of the time produced an impact on the authorship, style and content of this work. In order for you the reader to better appreciate and connect with this book, it is therefore important to have some context on world events during this timeframe. To this end, we have included a detailed events calendar for the early 20th Century for your reference.

Please give consideration in particular to the era around 1909, the year in which this work was first published.

Disclaimer: Some scenes throughout history may not be suitable for children, for example, in relation to war or violence. Please use your own discretion before reading this section to your child or allowing your child to read it.

1900 The United States, Japan, and Europe sent soldiers to China in order to rescue citizens and put a stop to the Boxer Rebellion. Angry troops march through the streets of Beijing, attacking everyone they suspect of being a Boxer. They cause injury to and pillage innocent Chinese.

1900 Germany is the world's most literate country. Germany possessed a qualified workforce, experienced farmers, and skilled military personnel. Britain, France, Norway, Sweden, and Australia all had high literacy rates, whereas China, India, Africa, and Islamic countries all had poor rates.

In 1800, there were a billion people. By 1900, there were 1.7 billion

1901 A new century begins, characterized by harsh working conditions and Europe's nationalism versus imperialism.

Imperialism was encouraged by the aristocracy and the Church in Europe. Emperor Franz Joseph of Austria-Hungary ruled with an ethical ethos.

1902 On this day in history, Vladimir Lenin, the Russian Marxist, celebrated his 32nd birthday. What Is to Be Done, which was published in May, is his new work. He accuses his socialist father, 52-year-old Eduard Bernstein, of betraying Marx's scientific socialism in the book. By using failed predictions, Bernstein tries to modernize Marxism. Lenin is unshakable and believes there are none.

1903 The California agricultural contracting firm was established by growers (WACC). WACC, according to the Japanese-Mexican Labor Association (JMLA), intentionally decreased salaries. According to JMLA, WACC forced workers to pay double commissions and purchase goods at inflated prices.

1904 In early August, the German naval and military attachés in London were concerned about a possible British navy attack. He thinks the attachés because his British family has flouted regulations. King Edward VII (a monarch opposed to the Kaiser) wants war, according to him. Germany's navy is always prepared and awaits orders. The majority of people were misled.

1905 The San Francisco city school board relocated Japanese pupils to the city's sole Asian institution because "our youngsters were not put in a position where their ideas might be influenced by Mongolian kids."

1906 Upton Sinclair's masterpiece The Jungle was published in the United States by Doubleday. The plot revolves around a hardworking immigrant family striving for the "American Dream." The meat packing sector deception and fraud were exposed in the book. Despite industry lobbyists' efforts to weaken it, legislation with real government inspections and limitations was passed, despite their protests. Sinclair was furious about how little socialism there was in this edition.

The Japanese decision to disband the Korean military in 1907 triggered a rebellion among the troops, and Japan responded with violence.

In 1908, the Hoover Company takes control of the US manufacturing rights to James M. Spangler's new upright portable vacuum cleaner.

In 1909, President Taft and his attorney general agreed on a planned federal income tax plan.

Slavery had been permitted in China for about 3000 years before it was made illegal in 1910.

In 1911, after completing his doctorate at the Zurich Polytechnic Institute and moving to Germany, Albert Einstein enrolls at Karl-Ferdinand University in Prague. He will be instructing mechanics and kinetic heat theory during the summer term.

In 1912, the United States seizes Tientsin, China, to safeguard America's interests. Until 1938, an American force will be stationed in the country.

The Sixteenth Amendment was approved in 1913, allowing Congress to levy taxes on "incomes from whatever source derived without regard to apportionment among the states, census, or enumeration."

On June 28, 1914, Archduke Franz Ferdinand, heir to the Austro-Hungarian crown and Inspector General of the armed forces, goes on a trip to Bosnia without the security usually provided against assassins. Following is an occurrence that is generally considered to have triggered World War I. Before Gavrilo Princip shot him and his wife in Sarajevo, Bosnia, Ferdinand remarked that everything is in God's hands. The elderly Habsburg emperor, Franz Joseph, breathes a sigh of relief. He was not looking forward to seeing Ferdinand take over from him as ruler of Austria-Hungary.

In 1914, the Colorado National Guard killed a tent colony of 1,200 striking miners at Ludlow, which became known as the Ludlow Massacre.

The Telephone's First Coast-to-Coast Call (San Francisco to New York City) is made with a newly designed vacuum tube amplifier (1915).

The first successful blood transfusion was done by the Royal Army Medical Corps in 1916.

Mexico supports Germany against the United States in January 1917, and Germany issues the secret Zimmermann Telegram, proposing the return of Mexican border territories seized after the US-Mexico War. The telegraph is published by the United States government following its interception by British intelligence.

With the Sedition Act of 1918, the United States Congress widened the scope of the 1917 Espionage Act. Criticism of the administration or military campaign is considered treasonous.

On November 11, 1918, the armistice was signed at Le Francport near Compiegne, bringing to an end more than four years of gruesome conflict and millions of fatalities. The cannons on the Western Front fell silent, signaling the end of World War I's land, sea, and air battles between the Allies and Germany's last remaining opponent. Despite the fact that fighting continued elsewhere, the armistice between Germany and the Allies was the first step toward ending World War I. People from Germany emigrate to America for the most exuberant party in history. General Pershing is unhappy because he expected to fight in Germany.

In Paris, a peace conference to end World War I is held in 1919. There will be 27 nations in attendance, but Germany will not be among them.

In 1920, the United States Senate objects to joining the League of Nations. The requirement in the League Covenant that a member be helped if he or she had been assaulted elsewhere was condemned. Warren G. Harding became the 29th President of the United States in 1921. He continues: "We can now see both free and safe." He concludes with, "I am confident that Congress and the Executive Branch will support any necessary government action to help restore and stimulate growth."

The Communist Party of the Soviet Union selects Joseph Stalin as General Secretary in 1922. At Stalin's request, Lenin created this position in 1921.

In 1923, the United States finishes withdrawing its last forces from Germany, leaving the Ehren Breitstein Fortress vacant.

A constitution is passed by the Soviet Congress in April 1924. It was a treaty that merged three countries into one: Belorussian, Ukrainian, and Transcaucasian.

In March of 1925, the "Monkey Trial" in Tennessee came to a conclusion. John T. Scopes was convicted of teaching evolution in violation of state law. He is fined $100.

1926 In May, the pound is overvalued as it is on the gold standard. Coal exports were decreasing, and mine owners sought to reduce wages. Labor unrest was on the rise. London was in a state of terror as a result of an BBC radio drama depicting a workers' revolution.

On July 10, 1927, the first transatlantic radio phone conversation took place between New York and London.

Another fruitless bomb attack against Italian fascism took place in Buenos Aires, Argentina, on May 28, 1928. The explosion kills 43 people and wounds 22 others.

1929 The Soviet Union, Poland, Estonia, Romania, and Latvia sign the Litvinov Protocol in Moscow on March 19th.

"Words were wonderful, but weapons, machine guns, ships, and aeroplanes were more elegant," Mussolini told his fascist blackshirts in 1930. (Smoke from Humans)

In 1931, the League of Nations condemns Poland's treatment of Germans in Upper Silesia.

1932 The Stimson Doctrine, which stated that the United States would not recognize changes imposed by force in Manchuria, was on the rise at this time.

1933 The Oxford University undergraduates argue if "this House would ever fight for king and country." The decision is in favor. This is a common viewpoint at American universities.

1934 The USSR is concerned about a revitalized Germany. Poland has been added to the non-aggression agreement, and an enormous military buildup has begun.

1935In the United States, civil aircraft are prohibited from flying over the White House.

1936 Sweden has risen from the ashes. Since 1929, its industrial output has increased by more than twofold, and unemployment has plummeted to 5% (compared to 15% in the

United States).

1937 "I know some of you believe I should be harsher on Hitler than I am, but have you considered the prospect of a bomb on your breakfast table?" Mr. Baldwin, British Prime Minister, on appeasement.

1938 Adolf Hitler was made Supreme Commander of the Armed Forces (Oberkommando).

1939 The United Kingdom and France had their final ultimatum to Hitler: get out of Poland, or else. World War II begins.

At the Reichstag in 1939, Hitler declared that if "international Jewish financiers" were successful in restarting World War II, the "Jewish race in Europe would be destroyed." The Reichstag members applaud.

1940 The current NKVD chief Navrenty Beria is prosecuting the former NKVD chief Nicholai Yezhov. Beria urges Yezhov to confess so that Stalin may be saved. Because of his politeness, Yezhov declines.

5000 The British Royal Navy invades Greece in 1941. In his diary, Goebbels notes: "He and his coworkers are hoping for peace. Late. The game must be finished."

On December 7, 1941, Japan attacks the Netherlands and sends troops to Indonesia and Borneo. Japan also deploys troupes to New Guinea.

At a ten-day conference in Casablanca, President Roosevelt, Prime Minister Churchill, General Giraud, and General De Gaulle all agreed that the war must come to an end with the unconditional surrender of all hostile nations.

1944 The American medical researcher Oswald Avery (1877-1955) discovered DNA, the nucleic acid responsible for all known living species' development and function.

1945 On the Philippine island of Luzon, around 100 US soldiers and about 400 Filipino guerrilla fighters liberate 531 American POWs. 26 rebels and one US soldier are slain.

On May 8, 1945, a week after Adolf Hitler's suicide, the Allies acknowledged Germany's defeat.

On May 8, 1945, Winston Churchill declared VE Day as the

end of WWII in Europe.

Street parties were held in various towns throughout the United Kingdom to commemorate the conclusion of World War II.

Despite the fact that the conflict in the Far East had been declared over, more people died.

Despite the harsh conditions, some Japanese soldiers continued to fight as long as they could. It lasted a few more months after that.

The surrender of Japan was swift and unconditional, with the Soviet Union, the United States, Britain, China, Australia and other countries signing an armistice. The atomic bombs were dropped on August 6th. This day is now recognized as Victory over Japan Day (VJ).

The formal surrender documents were not completed until September 2nd. On September 2, 1945, six years and one day after the Nazis invaded Poland, the surrender was held on the USS Missouri in Tokyo Bay. World War II came to a close.

1946 Stalin informs the people of the Soviet Union that his government will continue to fight for peace and progress. "Mr. Churchill has now assumed the role of a war firebrand."

1947 The United States criticized Poland's Provisional Government for "having failed to observe its sacred obligations" to hold free and unrestricted elections as required by the Yalta and Potsdam Treaties.

A communist Interior Minister was compelled to submit a report on the politicisation of the police to the Czechoslovak parliament.

1949 Cardinal Mindszenty was imprisoned for the remainder of his life in Hungary for treason. He "confessed" to his crimes. More individuals were convinced of the moral bankruptcy of Communist regimes.

1950 The United States State Department was said to have 205 communists in it, according to Senator Joe McCarthy of Wisconsin.

This concludes the historical context.

Made in the USA
Thornton, CO
08/31/24 08:24:08

cbdc391e-6ee9-4dce-ab2d-073dde196a1fR02